THE GENESIS TRILOGY

Follow God's Word and It Will Be All Right

THE GENESIS TRILOGY

Follow God's Word and It Will Be All Right

BY

TONY WATERMAN

www.bookstandpublishing.com

Published by
Bookstand Publishing
Pasadena, CA 91101
4937_3

Copyright © 2022 by Tony Waterman
All rights reserved. No part of this publication may be reproduced or transmitted in any form or by any means, electronic or mechanical, including photocopy, recording, or any information storage and retrieval system, without permission in writing from the copyright owner.

ISBN 978-1-956785-31-9

Preface

I, Tony Waterman, was born in Alexandria, VA, in 1964 to single mom, Ms. Mildred Waterman, who was sixteen years old at the time. As a young man I learned about God and went to church with my Grandmother, Mrs. Lillian Waterman, who was the inspiration for this book. She believed that we here on Earth were not the only people that existed, and that there were other people in other universes that existed that had not committed sin like Adam and Eve committed on this Earth. Lillian raised me because my mom, Mildred experienced a hard life because of her father, Mr. Elijah Waterman's, bad choices of drinking, living from pillar to post, and domestic abuse.

Elijah was a brilliant man and earned wages laying bricks and ran a bootlegging business to provide his family a good life, however, for some reason he did not do that. To this day, I never understood that choice. Lillian did the best she could in raising a young Black boy, essentially all alone. I did not experience the traditional family unit, but I knew that there was power in a strong family unit. I saw my aunt, Mrs. Virginia Waterman Brower and her husband, Mr. Carl Brower as role models because they lived in a house and I lived in an apartment and was inspired to live in and own a house one day because of them. Mildred and Lillian both had impeccable memories. They could remember when a situation happened and could tell you in what year, month, and day the event happened even if the event occurred twenty, or more years ago. I was amazed at that ability and I inherited some of that memory and used that to become an Electrical Engineer and graduate from Howard University.

As far as I can remember from four years old, Mildred was institutionalized at St. Elizabeth Hospital until her death on February 14, 1994, and I never knew my dad. Everything that I learned that has made me successful in life, I learned from my grandmother, Lillian or on the streets. I often say, "I have a Bachelor of Science Electrical Engineering from Howard University, but I have a Ph.D. from the streets." I am happily married to Mrs. Kimberlyn Waterman and we have four beautiful children. I have grown as a husband and father over the years. I have also grown closer with God as my walk has strengthened. I am spiritual and my love for God and the desire to understand and read the word has been something that has been placed in my heart. That is why it was important for me to author this book. I want the readers who are believers and non-believers to read *The Genesis Trilogy*, but to also think about what could be different if Adam and Eve made different choices and how maintaining a strong family bond impacts your family for generations to come.

The Genesis Trilogy looks at three different universes with their own Adam and Eve. There are two imaginary universes and another universe that parallels the book of Genesis as we know it today. In each universe, God created an Adam and Eve with each taking different paths as they interact with Satan as the Serpent and the Tree of Knowledge of Good and Evil. Their paths of destiny take divergent directions and have consequences based upon the choices they make. The stories of each universe center around the Head of the house, the father, and how his choices impact the future of his family for generations. Follow God's word and it will be all right!

Contents

Preface v

Introduction ix

Chapter 1: The Serpent 1

Chapter 2: Creation of the Trilogy Universes 3

Chapter 3: Universe 1 – Adam Leads Eve Astray 7

Chapter 4: Universe 2 – Eve Leads Adam Astray 11

Chapter 5: Universe 3 – Rejection of Satan by Adam and Eve 13

Chapter 6: Life Outside the Garden of Eden
(Universe 1 – Inclination for Sin) 15

Chapter 7: Life Outside the Garden of Eden
(Universe 2 – Parallel of Original Genesis) 39

Chapter 8: Life Inside the Garden of Eden
(Universe 3 – Rejection of Satan) 55

Chapter 9: Noah and Space Travel (Universe 3) 59

Chapter 10: Living with Guardian Angels (Universe 1) 63

Chapter 11: Living with Guardian Angels (Universe 2) 69

Chapter 12: Guardian Angels Return to Heaven 75

Introduction

The Genesis Trilogy looks at two different imaginary universes and another universe that parallels the book of Genesis as we know it today. In each universe God created an Adam and Eve with each taking different paths on following Gods word or not. They all interact with Satan as the Serpent and the Tree of Knowledge of Good and Evil. Their paths of destiny take on divergent directions and have consequences based upon the choices they make.

In Universe 1, Adam and Eve eat from the Tree of Knowledge of Good and Evil. Adam is a weak father figure and as a result he has a bad influence on his family. Adam influences Eve to eat from the Tree of Knowledge and Good and Evil, thus corrupts his wife, Eve; which is the opposite of the story told in Genesis; where Eve influences Adam. This universe explores the consequences of a weak father's influence on his family for generations. As we see too often in our society, families with a weak or absent fathers, often than not suffer for generations.

Universe 2 closely portrays the original story told in Genesis, with Adam being influenced by Eve to eat from the Tree of Knowledge of Good and Evil. In this universe, Adam and Eve and their descendants are given an opportunity to choose between good and evil and their salvation. God has given us a choice to accept God or accept the wages of sin, death. In addition, Guardian Angels from Universe 3, have blended into their society to help educate and guide them to make better choices for their life and salvation. Today, God has given us the opportunity to accept Christ as our Lord and Savior.

In Universe 3, Adam and Eve did not eat from the Tree of Knowledge of Good and Evil. This universe explores what life could have been like without sin in the world and attempts to portray how life could be in Heaven. In this universe, Adam is a strong father figure and Head of his family and demonstrates how a strong father figure has a positive impact on his family for generations. Since they are without sin, God allows them to travel to other universes as Guardian Angels to help universes 1 and 2, that have sinned to make better choices for their salvation. It is beyond our imagination, but if we could imagine life without sin and how glorious that would be. There would not be any sickness, death, jealousy, hate, crime, or evil. All the people would be beautiful, all would be naked, and not ashamed of their nakedness. Husbands would love their wives' as they loved themselves and wives would love and honor their husband. There would be mutual love and respect for each other and their neighbor.

Chapter 1:
The Serpent

This story begins with the Lord observing Satan traveling to and from universes, trying to deceive and destroy. One day, Angels came to present themselves before the Lord, and Satan also came with them. The Lord said to Satan, "Where have you come from?" Satan answered the Lord, "From roaming throughout the universes, going back and forth among them."

God's Discussion with Satan:

Satan said to the Lord, "I have had discussions with each of the Adam's and Eves' and they have interest in wisdom and knowledge."

The Lord said to Satan, "In one instance you are tempting the weaker vessel to get at the Head. In another instance you have seen that the Head is weak, and you are tempting him. If you do, I shall punish you according to each circumstance."

God has a Vision of Universe 1 and Sees the Following Scene:

Adam saw that the fruit of the tree was good for food, pleasing to the eye, and desirable for gaining wisdom. Eve said, "We are free to eat from any tree in the garden; but we must not eat from the Tree of Knowledge of Good and Evil, for when you eat from it you will certainly die, I don't want to die." Adam took some fruit from the Tree of Knowledge of Good and Evil and ate it, then convinced Eve to partake. Eve was a good woman and soul mate for Adam. She relied on her husband to be the Head of the family and ensure their well-being, but he corrupted her. As the Head, Adam has led Eve to be disobedient to God.

God was displeased at this scenario.

God has a Vision of Universe 2 and Sees the Following Scene:

Eve saw that the fruit of the tree was good for food, pleasing to the eye, and desirable for gaining wisdom. Eve said, "We are free to eat from any tree in the garden; but we must not eat from the Tree of Knowledge of Good and Evil, for when you eat from it you will certainly die, I don't want to die and don't believe I will." Eve took some fruit from the Tree of Knowledge and Good and Evil and ate it, then convinced Adam to partake. The weaker vessel, Eve, has convinced the Head, Adam, to be disobedient to God. Eve tempts Adam, and Adam partakes.

God was displeased at this scenario.

God has a Vision of Universe 3 and Sees the Following Scene:

Adam and Eve saw that the fruit of the Tree of Knowledge of Good and Evil was good for food, pleasing to the eye, and desirable for gaining wisdom. They decided to discuss the matter together as a family. Eve said, "It looks good, I would like to have wisdom." Adam, "You are right, but I don't want to die." Eve, said "You are right, husband, I don't want to die either." They were as one, husband and wife, as God had intended, stronger together, and they worked together as a family, and they rebuked Satan, the Serpent. They said to Satan, the Serpent, "Leave us you deceiver, liar, destroyer, and killer." They were allowed to remain in the Garden of Eden unaware of their nakedness and still obedient to God. Since Adam and Eve never died, they became Angels and so did their descendants.

God was pleased at this scenario.

Chapter 2:
Creation of the Trilogy Universes

As we look up into the sky we see the galaxies, stars, and planets and we wonder who, or what else is out there in that vast infinity of space.

In the beginning, God created the Heavens and the Earths. God has created many universes; however, we shall observe three parallel universes with three sets of Adam and Eve's; each has the choice of free will between good and evil; we shall imagine the consequences of their choices and actions.

And God said, "Let there be light," and there was light. God saw that the light was good, and he separated the light from the darkness. God called the light "day," and the darkness he called "night." And there was evening and there was morning – the first day.

And God said, "Let there be a vault between the waters to separate water from water." So, God made the vault and separated the water under the vault from the water above it. And it was so, God called the vault "Sky." – second day.

Then God said, "Let the land produce vegetation, plants, and trees, and it was so.

Then God said, "Let there be lights in the sky to separate day from night. God made two great lights, – the greater light to govern the day and the lesser light to govern the night. God saw that it was good.

Then God said, "Let the water teem with living creatures, and let birds fly above the Earth across the vault of the sky. God saw that it was good.

Then God said, "Let the land produce living creatures according to their kinds; the livestock, the creatures that move along the ground, and the wild animals according to their kind. God saw that it was good.

Then God said, "let us make mankind in our image, in our likeness, so that they may rule over the fish in the sea and the birds in the sky, over the livestock and all the wild animals, and over all the creatures that move along the ground."

So, God created mankind in his own image in the image of God he created them; male and female he created them. God blessed them and said to them, "Be fruitful and increase in number; fill the Earth and subdue it. Rule over the fish in the sea and over every living creature that moves on the ground.

By the seventh day God had finished the work he had been doing; so, on the seventh day, the Sabbath, he rested from all his work. Then God blessed the seventh day and made it holy because on it he rested from all the work of creating all that he had done.

God formed a man from the dust of the ground and breathed into his nostrils the breath of life, and the man became a living being, Adam. God has created three Adams in three different universes. Each has free will to make choices for his life.

For each universe, God had planted a garden in the east, Eden, and there he put Adam. God had made all kinds of trees grow out of the ground – trees that were pleasing to the eye and good for food.

In the middle of the Garden of Eden was the Tree of Life and the Tree of Knowledge of Good and Evil!

God took Adam and put him in the Garden of Eden to work it and take care of it. And God commanded Adam, "You are free to eat from any tree in the garden, but you must not eat from the Tree of

Knowledge of Good and Evil, for when you eat from it you will certainly die.

The Lord God said, "It is not good for the man to be alone. I will make a helper suitable for him. So, God caused each Adam to fall into a deep sleep; and while they were sleeping, he took one of their ribs and then closed the place with the flesh. Then the Lord God made a woman for each of them from the rib he had taken out of them, and he brought each woman to her man. Each man said, "This is now the bone of my bones and flesh of my flesh; she shall be called woman for she was taken out of man." God has created three women. God created an Eve for each one of the Adam's.

That is why man leaves his father and mother and is united to his wife, and they become one flesh. Adam and his wife, Eve, were both naked and they felt no shame on any of the universes.

THE GENESIS TRILOGY

Chapter 3:
Universe 1 – Adam Leads Eve Astray

Now the serpent was craftier than any of the wild animals the Lord God had created. He said to the woman, "Did God really say, 'You must not eat from any tree in the garden?'" The woman said to the serpent, "We may eat fruit from the trees in the garden, but God said, 'you must not eat fruit from the tree that is in the middle of the garden, and you must not touch it, or you will die.'"

"You will not certainly die," the serpent said to the woman. For God knows that when you eat from it your eyes will be opened, and you will be like God, knowing good and evil." When the woman saw that the fruit of the tree was good for food and pleasing to the eye and desirable for gaining wisdom, knowing good and evil. She said, "God has made life good for my husband and me. I do not want to know good and evil, for God has provided all that I need, but I will talk with my husband for he is the Head." Eve say's to Adam, "The serpent said, "You will not certainly die." For God knows that when you eat from it your eyes will be opened, and you will be like God, knowing good and evil." Adam saw that the fruit of the tree was good for food, pleasing to the eye, and desirable for gaining wisdom. Eve said, "We are free to eat from any tree in the garden; but we must not eat from the Tree of Knowledge of Good and Evil, for when you eat from it you will certainly die, I don't want to die." Eve was a good woman! With disregard to God, Adam took some fruit from the Tree of Knowledge of Good and Evil and ate it.

Now his eyes were open! He was now like God, knowing good and evil. He says to Eve, a good woman, "Now you see I am not dead." He now goes to Eve to give her some of the fruit and convinces her to eat. She was reluctant because she knew better, however, she loves her husband and follows his lead because he is the Head and she eats the forbidden fruit. Now they both are like God, knowing good and evil. Now, they realized they are naked; so, they sewed fig leaves together and made coverings for themselves.

Adam and Eve heard the Lord God walking in the Garden, and they hid from the Lord among the trees of the garden. The Lord God called to Adam, "Where are you?" Adam answered, "I heard you in the garden, and I was afraid because I was naked; so, I hid. God said, "Who told you that you were naked? Have you eaten from the tree I commanded you not to eat from?"

Adam said, "I have eaten from the Tree of Knowledge of Good and Evil and I now know good and evil. I also gave fruit to my woman, and she has eaten it also."

The Lord said to Adam, "You are the Head, and have not obeyed, and you have corrupted your woman, you have tempted your wife, the flesh of your flesh, bone of your bones. Your role is to honor her, but you have led her astray." "For this, cursed is the ground because of you; through painful toil you will eat food from it all the days of your life and you shall surely die. It will produce thorns and thistles for you, and you will eat the plants of the field.

By the sweat of your brow, you will eat your food until you return to the ground, since from it you were taken; for dust you are and to dust you will return." "You shall suffer the pain and agony of living longer than many of your children because you are weak of mind, body, and spirit and the apple does not fall far from the tree." One of the most painful things in life a parent can experience is the loss of a child!

God said to Eve, "I will make your childbearing severe; with painful labor you will give birth to children. Eve, I do not blame you

Universe 1 – Adam Leads Eve Astray

because your husband is the Head and he knew better, though, you knew better and decided to disobey."

God said to Adam and Eve, "You shall live one hundred years less than expected and die with a weak legacy and weak offspring. You come from the dust and shall return to the dust."

God said, "The man should leave his father and mother and is united to his wife, and they become one flesh. In this case, the flesh is sick because Adam has corrupted the flesh of his flesh and the bone of his bones." God said, "There is a cure for this sickness and that is through me."

Adam named his wife Eve because she would become the mother of all the living.

The LORD God made garments of skin for Adam and Eve and clothed them. And the LORD God said, "The man has now become like one of us, knowing good and evil. He must not be allowed to reach out his hand and take also from the Tree of Life and eat and live forever."

THE GENESIS TRILOGY

Chapter 4:
Universe 2 – Eve Leads Adam Astray

The serpent was craftier than any of the wild animals the Lord God had made. He said to the woman, "Did God really say, "You must not eat from any tree in the garden?

The woman said to the serpent, "We may eat fruit from the tree in the garden, but God did say, "You must not eat fruit from the tree that is in the middle of the garden, and you must not touch it, for you will die." You will not certainly die, " the serpent said to Eve. For God knows that when you eat from it your eyes will be opened, and you will be like God, knowing good and evil.

Eve saw that the fruit of the tree was good for food, pleasing to the eye, and desirable for gaining wisdom, she took some and ate it. Now her eyes were opened! She was now like God knowing good and evil. She now goes to Adam to give him some of the fruit. Adam saw that the fruit of the tree was good for food and pleasing to the eye, and desirable for gaining wisdom. Adam said, "We are free to eat from any tree in the garden; but we must not eat from the Tree of Knowledge of Good and Evil, for when you eat from it you will certainly die. I do not want to die; however, Adam took some fruit from the Tree of Knowledge of Good and Evil and ate it.

Adam said, "We are like God knowing good and evil and we shall surely die." They realized they were naked; so they sewed fig leaves together and made coverings for themselves.

Adam and Eve heard the Lord God walking in the Garden, and they hid from the Lord among the trees of the garden. The Lord God called to Adam, "Where are you?" Adam answered, "I heard you in the garden, and I was afraid because I was naked; so, I hid. God said, "who told you that you were naked? Have you eaten from the tree I commanded you not to eat from?"

The man said, "The woman you put here with me—she gave me some fruit from the tree, and I ate it." Then the LORD God said to the woman, "What is this you have done?" The woman said, "The serpent deceived me, and I ate." So, the LORD God said to the Serpent, "Because you have done this, "Cursed are you above all livestock and all wild animals! You will crawl on your belly, and you will eat dust all the days of your life. And I will put enmity between you and the woman, and between your offspring and hers; he will crush your head, and you will strike his heel." To the woman he said, "I will make your pains in childbearing severe; with painful labor you will give birth to children. Your desire will be for your husband, and he will rule over you." To Adam he said, "Because you listened to your wife and ate fruit from the tree about which I commanded you, 'You must not eat from it,' "Cursed is the ground because of you; through painful toil you will eat food from it all the days of your life. It will produce thorns and thistles for you, and you will eat the plants of the field. By the sweat of your brow, you will eat your food until you return to the ground, since from it you were taken; for dust you are and to dust you will return."

Adam named his wife Eve because she would become the mother of all the living.

The LORD God made garments of skin for Adam and his wife and clothed them. And the LORD God said, "The man has now become like one of us, knowing good and evil. He must not be allowed to reach out his hand and take also from the Tree of Life and eat and live forever."

Chapter 5:
Universe 3 – Rejection of Satan by Adam and Eve

The serpent was craftier than any of the wild animals the Lord god had made. He said to the woman, "Did God really say, "You must not eat from any tree in the garden?

The woman said to the serpent, "We may eat fruit from the tree in the garden, but God did say, "You must not eat fruit from the tree that is in the middle of the garden, and you must not touch it, you will die." "You will not certainly die," the serpent said to Eve. "For God knows that when you eat from it your eyes will be opened, and you will be like God, knowing good and evil."

Eve saw that the fruit of the tree was good for food and pleasing to the eye, and desirable for gaining wisdom. She decided to discuss the matter with her husband, as a family. Eve said, "It looks good, I would like to have wisdom." Adam said, "You are right, but I don't want to die." Eve said, "You are right, husband, I don't want to die either." They were as one, as a strong family, and they rebuked the Serpent, and said, "Leave us you deceiver, liar, destroyer, and killer. We do not want to die. We want to live in the Garden of Eden in paradise as God has promised and delivered." Their eyes remained closed to good and evil, and they remained as husband and wife. They were naked and unashamed. They were not like God! They were obedient to God!

Adam and Eve heard the Lord God walking in the Garden, and they went to him. Adam said to God, "I heard you in the garden and wanted to tell you about what the Serpent said." The serpent said, "You will not certainly die. "For God knows that when you eat from it your eyes will be opened, and you will be like God, knowing good and evil."

Adam said, "I have not eaten from the Tree of Knowledge of Good and Evil and I do not know good and evil. I also have protected my wife, Eve, and she has "NOT" eaten from the Tree of Knowledge of Good and Evil."

The Lord said to Adam, "You are the Head, and have obeyed, and you have not corrupted your wife, your woman, you have not tempted the flesh of your flesh, bone of your bones. You honor her, and you have not led her astray." "For this, blessed is the ground because of you; you will eat food from it forever! It will produce the plants of the field forever. God said, "I am pleased." You have exemplified the life I intended mankind to live!

"Your children will be blessed, strong of mind, body, and spirit. The apple shall not fall far from the tree. They will be Guardian Angels to others who have fallen short of the will of God."

God said to Eve, "I will make your childbearing painless and beautiful. You will have many children and they shall honor and love you until the end of time."

God said to Adam and Eve, "You shall live in the Garden of Eden and your legacy will live forever and be wise and your descendants shall travel to and from universe to universe." You and your offspring shall be Guardian Angels to other universes. As Guardian Angels you shall visit and live among others that have sinned against God and provide guidance to them, however, unknown to them that you are a Guardian Angel. Since you have not sinned, your knowledge will be great amongst the sinners. You shall try to lead them to the path of righteousness. Some will accept this path and others will reject it because Satan has his followers. You shall assist them with all manners of human, social, medical, and scientific development over time because their intellect has been limited by sin.

God said, "The man should leave his father and mother and is united to his wife, and they become one flesh."

Chapter 6:

Life Outside the Garden of Eden (Universe 1 – Inclination for Sin)

Universe 1 Description:

This universe suffers from the consequences of a weak father and his family suffers from the consequences of a weak Head. Adam provided poor leadership to Eve and led her astray from God's direction. The wages of sin is death, and this universe will suffer because God's will is for strong a family structure that is led by a strong Head and father figure. In this universe, Adam's offspring will be weak, therefore, they will always struggle with right and wrong. Consequently, they will have challenges in life, in their relationships with family, friends, and spouse.

Universe 1 was filled with sin since Adam made a poor choice from the beginning with the bone of his bones and flesh of his flesh, Eve. No matter whatever the endeavor, their propensity for sin prevented them from overcoming their original sin from their father and they would always tend to their sinful ways. This was their generational curse. They were fornicators, rapists, murderers, thieves, and all sorts of deviants. Adam and his descendants thought this way of living was a way of life or a way of having a good time and having fun, but the wages of sin is death.

So the LORD God banished him from the Garden of Eden to work the ground from which he had been taken. After he drove man out, he placed on the east side of the Garden of Eden Cherubim and a flaming sword flashing back and forth to guard the way to the Tree of Life.

They began to learn how to farm and gather food, build shelters, make clothes, create tools and learn how to live off the land. Adam had sex with, as opposed to making love, to his wife Eve, and she became pregnant and gave birth to Cain. She experienced a great deal of pain and agony giving birth. She said, "With the help of the LORD I have brought forth a man." Later she gave birth to his brother Abel. Now Abel kept flocks and Cain worked the soil. In the course of time Cain brought some of the fruits of the soil as an offering to the LORD. And Abel also brought an offering – fat portions from some of the firstborn of his flock. The LORD looked with favor on Abel and his offering, but on Cain and his offering he did not look with favor. So Cain grew very angry, and his face was downcast. Then the LORD said to Cain, "Why are you angry? Why is your face downcast? If you do what is right, will you not be accepted? But if you do not do what is right, sin is crouching at your door; it desires to have you, but you must rule over it." Now Cain said to his brother Abel, "Let's go out to the field." While they were in the field, Cain attacked his brother Abel and tried to kill him, however, Abel was extraordinarily strong and fought back and killed Cain. Abel was much stronger than Cain and he did not have to kill Cain, but he killed him anyway. Cain begged for his life, but Abel slew him anyway. In this situation, Cain was an attempted murderer and Abel a murderer.

Then the LORD said to Abel, "Where is your brother Cain?" "I don't know," he replied. "Am I my brother's keeper?" The LORD said, "What have you done? Listen! Your brother's blood cries out to me from the ground. Now you are under a curse and driven from the ground, which opened its mouth to receive your brother's blood from your hand. When you work the ground, it will no longer yield any crops for you. You will be a restless wanderer on the Earth." Abel said to the LORD, "My punishment is more than I can bear. Today you are driving me from the land, and I will be hidden from your presence; I will be a restless wanderer on the Earth, and whoever finds me will try to kill me." But the LORD said to him, "Cain tried to kill you." Then

Life Outside the Garden of Eden (Universe 1 – Inclination for Sin)

the LORD put a mark on Abel so that however found him would know that he is a killer. So, Abel went out from the LORD's presence and lived in the land of Nod east of Eden.

Abel went out and found a wife and had sex with her. She became pregnant and gave birth to a son. His son had a son, and his son had a son and so on. Abel's descendants had multiple wives and multiple children. They were fornicators, rapists, and murderers. They were sinners and thought this was the way to live.

Adam had sex with his wife again, and she gave birth to a son named Seth. God has granted me a son in place of Cain since Abel killed him. Seth also had a son and he named him Enoch.

Normally at that time people would call on the name of the Lord for thanks, but they did not call on the name of the LORD because they were sinners.

When human beings began to increase in numbers on the Earth and daughters were born to them the sons of God saw that the daughters of humans were beautiful, and they fornicated with them as they chose. Then the LORD said, "My spirit will not contend with humans forever for they are mortal, and their numbers will be hundred years. This is twenty years short due to their proclivity for sin. In addition, living a sinful life shortens your life span because you are not treating your body like the temple that it is intended to be."

Abel was a killer until he was later killed by one of his own descendants.

Noah and the Flood:

Noah was trying to be a righteous man, trying to be blameless among the people of his time, and he tried to walk faithfully with God, however, he was affected by the generational curse of Adam. Noah had three sons: Shem, Ham, and Japeth.

Now the Earth was corrupt in God's sight and was full of violence and sin. God saw how corrupt the Earth had become, for all the people on Earth had corrupt ways. So God said to Noah, "I am going to put an end to all the people, for the Earth is filled with violence because of them. I am surely going to destroy them and the Earth. So, make yourself an Ark of cypress wood; make rooms in it and coat it with pitch inside and out. Noah did as God said, except he did **"NOT"** coat it with pitch inside and out. He only coated the outside because he did not think it really mattered that much since the outside was finished and he was tired. He thought to himself it looks good on the outside, so who would notice the inside. He was disobedient to God, which has consequences. This is how you are to build it: The Ark is to be three hundred cubits long, fifty cubits wide and thirty cubits high. Make a roof for it, leaving below the roof an opening one cubit high all around. Put a door in the side of the Ark and make lower, middle and upper decks. I am going to bring flood waters on the Earth to destroy all life under the Heavens, every creature that has the breath of life in it. But I will establish my covenant with you, and you will enter the Ark you and your sons and your wife and your sons' wives with you. You are to bring into the Ark two of all living creatures, male and female, to keep them alive with you. Two every kind of bird, of every kind of animal and of every kind of creature that moves along the ground will come to you to be kept alive. You are to take every kind of food and seed that is to be eaten and store it away as food for you and for them.

Noah did everything just as God commanded, **except** coat the inside of the Ark with pitch as instructed.

The LORD then said to Noah, "Go into the Ark, you and your whole family because I find you the most righteous in this generation." Take with you seven pairs of every kind of clean animal, a male and its mate, also seven pairs of every kind of bird, male and female to keep their various kinds alive throughout the Earth. Seven days from

Life Outside the Garden of Eden (Universe 1 – Inclination for Sin)

now I will send rain on the Earth for forty days and forty nights and I will wipe from the face of the Earth every living creature I have made.

When the flood waters came on the Earth, Noah and his wife and his sons and their wives entered the Ark to escape the waters of the flood. All the clean and unclean animals entered the Ark.

The flood kept coming on the Earth, and as the waters increased, lifted the Ark high above the Earth. The waters rose and increased greatly on the Earth and the Ark floated on the surface of the water. The entire Earth was covered with flood waters. Every living thing that moved on land perished. Only Noah was left and those with him in the Ark.

After 20 days and twenty nights the Ark developed a leak, due to it not being coated on the inside with pitch. This was the first sign of trouble for disobeying the Lord. This was the Lord sending Noah a warning of things to come! Noah quickly repaired the leak, but it was only a temporary fix because he did not confess of his sins to the Lord. On the 30th day, the Ark developed another leak and Noah repaired the leak. On the 40th day, the Ark developed multiple leaks. Now Noah and his family have become concerned about the leaks, and they asked, "Did you not build the Ark as God had commanded." Noah, replied "I did everything, except coat the inside of the Ark with pitch, however I did coat the outside." They replied, "Noah you did not follow God's plan." God has a plan for our lives and when we stray from that plan, we begin to experience leaks in our lives and we become unfulfilled. That unfulfillment often leads us try to fill that gap on our own, which leads to sin. Sometimes we try to fill that gap with sex, drinking, or drugs. The leaks on the Ark became increasingly troublesome and the Ark began to take on water because Noah and his family could not keep pace with repairing the leaks and bailing the water.

The waters rose and covered the mountains to a depth of more than fifteen cubits. Every living thing on the face of the Earth perished – birds, livestock, wild animals, creatures that swarm over the Earth, and all mankind. Everything on dry land that had the breath of life in its nostrils died. Only Noah was left and those with him in the Ark. Since the Ark was taking on water at a rapid rate some of the animals and creatures with him perished. Even Noah and his family had to fight for their lives due to the amount of incoming water. The Ark was sinking, as our lives sink when we do not follow the word and instruction of God. Noah was not a swimmer and almost drowned trying to repair the Ark. He was saved by his son Shem. Shem was strong and was able to pull his father from the depths and saved him. Ham and Japeth were feverously trying to save the Ark and as many of the animals they could.

The waters flooded the Earth for one-hundred and fifty days.

But God remembered Noah and all the wild animals and the livestock that were with him in the Ark, and he sent a wind over the Earth, and as the waters receded and Noah and all who were with him survived except those few animals that drowned on the Ark. The animals that drowned on the Ark became extinct, since they were the only living species of that animal. Noah learned a valuable lesson from that experience, follow God's commands and you can break the generational curse if you cleave to God and recognize the things you do have impact on others. It is there for you to see; you just have to open your eyes and want to see. On the seventh day of the seventh month the Ark came to rest on the mountains of Ararat. The waters continued to recede until the tenth month, and on the first day of the tenth month the tops of the mountains became visible.

Then, after forty days Noah sent out a raven, and it kept flying back and forth until the water had dried up from the Earth. Then he sent out a dove to see if the water had receded from the surface of the ground. The dove could find nowhere to perch because there was

Life Outside the Garden of Eden (Universe 1 – Inclination for Sin)

water all over the surface of the Earth; so, it returned to Noah in the Ark. He waited seven more days and sent the dove out again. When the dove returned, there in its beak was a freshly plucked olive leaf! Then Noah knew that the water was receding from the Earth. He waited seven more days and sent the dove out again, but this time it did not return to him. This while still contending with leaks on the Ark. They were exhausted repairing the Ark on a continual basis.

By the first day of the first month of Noah's six hundred and first year, the water had dried up from the Earth. Noah then removed the covering from the Ark and saw that the surface of the ground was dry, By the twenty seventh day of the second month the Earth was completely dry. Then God said to Noah, "Come out of the Ark, you and your wife and your sons and their wives'. Bring out every kind of living creature that is with you – the birds, then animals, and all the creatures that move along the ground and all the birds everything that moves on land – came out of the Ark, one kind after another." The animals that died along the trip will never walk on the Earth again due to Noah's disobedience. Then Noah built an altar to the Lord and, taking some of all the clean animals and clean birds, he sacrificed burnt offerings on it. The Lord smelled the pleasing aroma and said in his heart: "Never again will I curse the ground because of humans, even though every inclination of the human heart is evil from childhood. And never again will I destroy all living creatures as I have done.

As long as the Earth endures, seedtime and harvest, cold and heat, summer and winter, day and night, will never cease."

God's Covenant with Noah:

Even though Noah disobeyed, God still blessed Noah and his sons, saying to them, "Be fruitful and increase in number and fill the Earth. The fear and dread of you will fall on all the beasts of the Earth, and on all the birds in the sky, on every creature that moves along the ground, and on all the fish in the sea; they are given into your hands. Everything that lives and moves about will be food for you. Just as I gave you the green plants, I now give you everything.

But you must not eat meat that has its lifeblood still in it. And for your lifeblood I will surely demand an accounting. I will demand an accounting from every animal. And from each human being too, I will demand an accounting for the life of another human being. Whoever sheds human blood, by humans shall their blood be shed; for in the image of God has God made mankind.

Then God established a covenant with Noah and his sons and their descendants. Never again will all life be destroyed by the waters of a flood; never again will there be a flood to destroy the Earth. I have set my rainbow in the clouds, and it will be the sign of the covenant between me and the Earth. Whenever I bring clouds over the Earth and the rainbow appears in the clouds, I will remember my covenant between me and you and all living creatures of every kind. Never again will the waters become a flood to destroy all life.

The sons of Noah who came out of the Ark were Shem, Ham, and Japheth. From them came the people who were scattered over the whole Earth. These are the descendants of Adam, who led Eve into sin. These are the decedents of Adam, the weak Head and Father!

Noah a man of the soil, proceeded to plant a vineyard. When he drank some of its wine, he became drunk and lay uncovered inside his tent. Noah would get drunk too often, which led to him to neglecting his family by not producing enough food to regularly feed his family or providing a stable home or shelter. His drinking had an extremely negative impact on his family, which impacted his family for generations to come. The generational curse again! He was affected by a generational curse, and he knew how to break the generational curse. He did not do that and created his own generational curse for his descendants! His sons had issues dealing with their wives and children as a result. Their wives did not respect their husbands and the children did not respect their parents.

Ham, the father of Canaan, saw his father naked and told his two brothers outside. But Shem and Japheth thought about taking a garment and laying it across their shoulders, then walk in backwards and cover their father's naked body, but instead they decided to have fun and laugh at Noah. They looked at Noah's naked body and made fun of him. They did not honor or respect their father as they should have.

When Noah awoke from his wine and found out what his sons had done to him, he said, "Cursed be to all of them." This was in addition to the generational curse!

He also said, "May you all be damned! Praise be to the Lord, the God of Shem!"

The words a father speaks to his children have profound effects! His words could either build them up or tear them down emotionally and spiritually. A father should always speak words of encouragement to his children and build their self-esteem up as best as possible. He should spend quality time with his children and wife to build a strong family unit. This will inspire confident children, so that when they go out into the world, they can deal with the challenges that life presents. However, in his rage he tore them down. No matter how old, children are always looking for acceptance and approval from their parents, especially their father. Noah should have explained and taught his sons that what they did was wrong and provided guidance to them so that they would know how to manage difficult situations and be respectful to their parents so that their days on Earth would be long. A father's blessing or condemnation will have impact on future generations. Children need affirmation and a sense of purpose from their parents and a father's blessing is priceless for generations to come.

After the flood Noah Lived 250 years. Noah lived a total of 850 years, and then he died. This is one hundred years shorter than he should have lived due to his disobedience to God and his offspring suffered due to his negligence to his family.

The Tower of Babel:

Now the entire world had one language and a common speech. As people moved eastward, they found a plain in Shinar and settled there. They said to each other, "Come let's make bricks and bake them thoroughly." They used brick instead of stone, and tar for mortar. They said, "Come let us build ourselves a city with a tower that reaches into the Heavens, so that we may make a name for ourselves; otherwise, we will be scattered over the face of the whole Earth. They wanted to be like God and not need God! They showed pride and arrogance, which God did not like.

But the Lord came down to see the city and the tower the people were building. The Lord said, "If as one people speaking the same language, they have begun to do this, then nothing they plan to do will be impossible for them. The Lord confused their language so they could not understand each other. So, the Lord scattered them from there over all the Earth, and they stopped building the city. That is why it was called Babel. This caused great confusion among the people. Since they were prone to sin, people of different languages could not understand or communicate with each other, therefore, they often had fighting and wars between them. Satan enjoyed this confusion greatly!

The Call of Abram:

The Lord had said to Abram, "Go from your country, your people and your father's household to the land I will show you. I will make you into a great nation, and I will bless you; I will make your name great, and you will be a blessing. I will bless those who bless you, and whoever curses you I will curse; and all peoples on Earth will be blessed through you.

Life Outside the Garden of Eden (Universe 1 – Inclination for Sin)

So, Abram went, as the Lord had told him; and Lot went along with him. Abram was seventy-five years old when he set out from Harran. He took his wife Sarai, his nephew Lot, all the possessions they had accumulated and the people they had acquired in Harran, and they set out for the land of Canaan, and they arrived there.

Abram traveled through the land as far as the site of the great tree of Morehat Shechem. At that time the Canaanites were in the land. The Lord appeared to Abram and said, "To your offspring I will give this land." So, he built an altar there to the Lord, who had appeared to him.

From there he went on toward the hills east of Bethel and pitched his tent, with Bethel on the west and Ai on the east. There he built an altar to the Lord and called on the name of the Lord.

Then Abram set out and continued toward the Negev.

Abram in Egypt:

Now there was a famine in the land and Abram went down to Egypt to live there for a while because the famine was severe. As he was about to enter Egypt, he said to his wife Sarai. "I know what a beautiful woman you are. When the Egyptians see you, they will say, "This is his wife. Then they will kill me, but will let you live. Say you are my sister, so that I will be treated well for your sake and my life will be spared because of you."

When Abram came to Egypt, the Egyptians saw that Sarai was indeed an incredibly beautiful woman. And when Pharaoh's officials saw her, they praised her to Pharaoh, and she was taken into his palace. He treated Abram well for her sake, and Abram acquired sheep and cattle, male and female donkeys, male and female servants, and camels.

But the Lord inflicted serious diseases on Pharaoh and his household because of Abram's wife Sarai. So Pharaoh summoned

Abram. "What have you done to me?" he said. Why didn't you tell me she was your wife? Why did you say, "She is my sister, so that I took her to be my wife? Now then, here is your wife. Take her and go! Then Pharoah gave orders about Abram to his men, and they sent him on his way, with his wife and everything he owned. Abram said, "You can have her, I can get another wife." To say this, Abram did not love and respect his wife as bone of his bones and flesh of his flesh. A husband should always love, respect, and cleave to his wife. Pharoah rejected her and his offer!

Abram and Lot Separate:

So, Abram went up from Egypt to Negeve with his wife and everything he owned, and Lot went with him. Abram had become very wealthy in livestock and in silver and gold.

From Negev he went from place to place until he came to Bethel, to the place between Bethel and Ai where his tent had been earlier and where he had first built an altar. There Abram called on the name of the Lord.

Now Lot, who was moving about with Abram, also had flocks, herds, and tents. But the land could not support them while they stayed together, for their possessions were so great that they were not able to stay together. They began quarreling, fighting, and killings arose between Abram's herders and Lot's. The Canaanites and Perizzities were also living in the land at that time.

So Abram said to Lot, "Let's not have any quarreling, fighting, and killings between you and me or between your herders and mine, for we are close relatives. Is not the whole land before you? Let's part company. If you go to the left, I'll go to the right; If you to the right I'll go to the left."

Lot looked around and saw that the whole plain of the Jordan toward Zoar was well watered, like the garden of the Lord, like the land of Egypt. So, Lot chose for himself the whole plain of the Jordan

Life Outside the Garden of Eden (Universe 1 – Inclination for Sin)

and set out toward the east. The two men parted company. Abram lived in the land of Canaan, while Lot lived among the cities of the plain and pitched his tents near Sodom. Later, Lot decided that he wanted to live in the land of Canaan, which is not what the two men agreed upon. Jealousy had started to set in the heart of Lot. Now the people of Sodom were wicked and were sinning against the Lord. Lot observed the people of Sodom's wickedness and sinning and was influenced by their behavior and decided to try to take Abram's land and belongings. This was all due to greed and jealousy. Lot also engaged in sexual immorality with the people of Sodom.

The Lord said to Abram after Lot had parted from him, "Look around from where you are, to the north and south to the east and west. All the land that you see I will give to you and your offspring forever. I will make your offspring like the dust of the Earth, so that if anyone could count the dust, then your offspring could be counted. Go, walk through the length and breadth of the land, for I am giving it to you."

So, Abram went to live near the great trees of Mamre at Hebron, where he pitched his tents. There he built an altar to the Lord.

Lot and his men attacked Abram to take his land and his belongings, however, he was not aware of the Lord's promise to Abram about the land. Therefore, what the Lord has planned for you no man can take away. With the Lord's blessing Abram and his men defeated Lot and his men, killing many of them. Abram said to Lot, "You are a close relative, why have you attacked me?" Lot said, "He was influenced by the people of Sodom, but please forgive him for his misgivings." This lets you know that the people you let in your life have influences over you that sometimes you are not even aware of, therefore, keep company with people of good spirit. Abram, said "You are and always will be my relative, but not as close as before, but I will always be with you."

Abram Rescues Lot:

At the time when Amraphel was King of Shinar, Arioch King of Ellasar, Kedorlaomer King of Elam and Tidal King of Goyim, these Kings went to war against Bera King of Sodom, Birsha King of Gomorrah, Shinab King of Admah, Shemeber King of Zeboyim and the King of Bela. All these latter Kings joined forces in the valley of Sidim. For twelve years they had been subject to Kedorlaomer, but in the thirteenth year they rebelled.

In the fourteenth year, Kedorlaomer and the Kings allied with him went out and defeated the Rephaites in Ashteroth Karnaim, the Zuzites in Ham, the Emites in Shaveh Kirathaim and the Herites in the hill country of Seir as far as El Paran near the desert. They turned back and went to En Mishpat and they conquered the whole territory of the Amalekites, as well as the Amorites who were living in Hazezon Tamar.

Then the King of Sodom, and the King of Gomorrah, the King of Admah, the King of Zeboyim and the King of Bela marched out and drew up their battle lines in the Valley of siddim against Kerdorlaomer King of Elam, Tidal King of Goyim, Amraphel King of Shinar and Arioch Kings of Ellasar – four Kings against five. Now the Valley of Siddim was full of tar pits, and when Kings of Sodom and Gomorrah fled, some of the men fell into them and the rest fled to the hills. The four Kings seized all the goods of Sodom and Gomorrah and all their food; then they went away. They also carried off Abram's nephew Lot and his possessions, since he was living in Sodom.

A man who had escaped, came, and reported this to Abram the Hebrew. Now Abram was living near the great trees of Mamre the Amorite, a brother of Eshkol and Aner, all of whom were allied with Abram. When Abram heard that his relative had been taken captive, he called out the 318 trained men born in his household and went in pursuit as far as Dan. During the night Abram divided his men to

Life Outside the Garden of Eden (Universe 1 – Inclination for Sin)

attack them and he routed them, pursuing them as far as Hobah, north of Damascus. He recovered all the goods and brought back his relative, Lot, and his possessions, together with the women and the other people.

After Abram returned from defeating Kedorlaomer and the Kings allied with him, the King of Sodom came out to meet him in the Valley of Shaveh.

Then Melchizedek King of Salem offered bread and wine. He was priest of God most high, and he blessed Abram, saying,

"Blessed be Abram by God Most High, Creator of Heaven and Earth, and praise be to God Most High, who delivered your enemies into your hand."

Then Abram gave him a tenth of a tenth of everything, but in his heart, he knew he should have given him a tenth, but greed was in his heart!

The King of Sodom said to Abram, "Give me the people and keep the goods for yourself." But Abram said to the King of Sodom, "With raised hand I have sworn an oath to the Lord, God Most High, Creator of Heaven and Earth, that I will accept nothing belonging to you, not even a thread or the strap of a sandal, so that you will never be able to say, I made Abram rich. I will accept nothing but what my men have eaten and the share that belongs to the men who went with me – to Aner, Eshkol, and Mamre. Let them have their share." The King of Sodom said to Abram, "You have only given me a tenth of tenth, but you know you should have given me a tenth. You already have taken from me."

The Lord's Covenant with Abram:

After this, the word of the Lord came to Abram in a vision:

"Do not be afraid, Abram. I am your shield, your very great reward."

But Abram said, "Sovereign Lord, what can you give me since I remain childless and the one who will inherit my estate is Eliezer of Damascus: And Abram said, "You have given me not children; so, a servant in my household will be my heir."

Then the word of the Lord came to him: "This man will not be your heir, but a son who is your own flesh and blood will be your heir. He took him outside and said, "Look up at the sky and count the stars – if indeed you can count them." Then he said to him, "So shall your offspring be."

Abram did not believe the Lord. He thought that he was old, and his wife was also too old and therefore, this could not happen for him. He did not believe that the Lord was righteous and could not lie.

He also said to him, "I am the Lord, who brought you out of Ur of the Chaldeans to give you this land to take possession of it."

So, the Lord said to him, "Bring me a heifer, a goat and a ram, each three years old, along with a dove and a young pigeon."

Abram was skeptical; however, he brought all these to him, cut them in two and arranged the halves opposite each other; the birds however, he did not cut in half. Then birds of prey came down on the carcasses, but Abram drove them away.

As the sun was setting, Abram fell into a deep sleep, and a thick and dreadful darkness came over him. Then the Lord said to him, "Know for certain that for four hundred years your descendants will be strangers in a country not their own and that they will be enslaved and mistreated there. But I will punish the nation they serve as slaves, and afterward they will come out with great possessions. You, however, will go to your ancestors in peace and be buried at a good old age. In the fourth generation your decedents will come back here, for the sin of the Amorites has not yet reached its full measure.

Life Outside the Garden of Eden (Universe 1 – Inclination for Sin)

When the sun had set and darkness had fallen, smoking firepot with a blazing torch appeared and passed between the pieces. On that day the Lord made a covenant with Abram and said, "To your descendants I give this land, from the Wadi of Egypt to the great river, the Euphrates – the land of the Kenites, Kenizzites, Repahites, Amorites, Canaanites, Girgashites, and Jebusites."

Hagar and Ishmael:

Now Sarai, Abram's wife, had borne him no children. But she said to Abram. "The Lord has kept me from having children. Go, sleep with my slave; perhaps I can build a family through her." Abram agreed to what Sari suggested because he had already been sleeping with her and other women and she was already with child. He remembered what the Lord, said, "Look up at the sky and count the stars – if indeed you can count them." Then he said to him, "So shall your offspring be." Abram didn't believe what the Lord had told him about Sarai and took it upon himself to produce his offspring. So, after Abram had been living in Canaan ten years, Sarai his wife took her Egyptian slave Hagar and gave her to her husband to be his wife, now he could sleep with her openly, instead of in hiding. He slept with Hagar under these conditions, but she was already with child by Abram.

When she knew she was pregnant, she began to despise her mistress. then Sarai said to Abram, "You are responsible for the wrong I am suffering. I put my slave in your arms, and now that she knows she is pregnant, she despises me. May the Lord judge between you and me."

"Your slave is in your hands," Abram said. "Do with her whatever you think best." Then Sarai plotted killing Hagar, but Abram would not let this happen, so she mistreated Hagar; so, she fled from her.

The angel of the Lord found Hagar near a spring in the desert; it was the spring that is beside the road the Shur.

And he said, "Hagar, slave of Sarai, where have you come from, and where are you going? I am running away from my mistress Sarai, she wants to kill me, "she answered.

Then the angel of the Lord told her, "Go back to your mistress and submit to her, and she will not kill you." The angel added, I will increase your descendants so much that they will be too numerous to count."

The angel of the Lord also said, "You are now pregnant, and you will give birth to a son. You shall name him Ishmael, for the Lord had heard of your misery. He will be a wild donkey of a man; his hand will be against everyone and everyone's hand against him, and he will live in hostility toward all his brothers.

She gave this name to the Lord who spoke to her: "You are the God who sees me," for she said, "I have now seen the One who sees me." That is why the well was called Beer Lahai Roi; it is still there, between Kadesh and Bered.

So, Hagar bore Abram a son, and Abram gave the name Ishmael to the son she had borne. Abram was eighty-six years old when Hagar bore him Ishmael.

The Covenant of Circumcision:

When Abram was ninety-nine years old, the Lord appeared to him and said, "I am God Almighty; walk before me faithfully and be blameless. Then I will make my covenant between me and you and will greatly increase your numbers. "

Abram fell face down, and God said to him, "As for me, this is my covenant with you; You will be the father of many nations. No longer will you be called Abram; your name will be *Abraham,* for I have made you a father of many nations. I will make you fruitful; I

Life Outside the Garden of Eden (Universe 1 – Inclination for Sin)

will make nations of you, and Kings will come from you. I will establish my covenant as an everlasting covenant between me and you and your descendants after you for the generations to come to be your God and the God of your descendants after you. The whole land of Canaan, where you and your descendants after you; and I will be their God."

Then God said to Abraham, "As for you, you must keep my covenant, you, and your descendants after you for the generations to come. This is my covenant with you and your descendants after you, the covenant you are to keep; Every male among you shall be circumcised. You are to undergo circumcision, and it will be the sign of the covenant between me and you. For the generations to come every male among you who is eight days old must be circumcised, including those born in your household or brought with money from a foreigner – those who are not your offspring. Whether born in your household or brought with your money, they must be circumcised. My covenant in your flesh is to be an everlasting covenant. Any uncircumcised male, who has not been circumcised in the flesh, will be cut off from his people; he has broken my covenant." Abraham did not keep his covenant, every male was not circumcised, especially foreigners that were not his offspring. Abraham's covenant with God only lasted a few generations because he was not obedient to God.

God also said to Abraham, "As for Sarai your wife, you are no longer to call her Sarai; her name will be Sarah. I will bless her, and she will surely bear you a son. I will bless her that she will be the mother of nations; Kings of peoples will come from her." Abraham still did not believe, he fell facedown; he laughed and said to himself, "Will a son be born to a man a hundred years old? Will Sarah bear a child at the age of ninety? And Abraham said to God, "If only Ishmael might live under your blessing?"

Then God said, "Yes, but your wife Sarah will bear you a son, and you will name your son Isaac. I will establish my covenant with him as an everlasting covenant for his descendants after him. And as for Ishmael, I have heard you; I will surely bless him; I will make him fruitful and will greatly increase his numbers. He will be the father of twelve rulers, and I will make him into a great nation.

But my covenant I will establish with Isaac, whom Sarah will bear to you by this time next year. When he had finished speaking with Abraham, God went up from him.

On that very day Abraham took his son Ishmael and all those born in his household, except those brought with his money, every male in his household, and circumcised them. God told him to circumcise them all including those brought with his money. Abraham was ninety-nine years old when he was circumcised, and his son Ishmael was thirteen; Abraham and his son Ishmael were both circumcised on that very day.

And every male in Abraham's household, including those born in his household, except brought from a foreigner, was circumcised with him.

The Three Visitors:

The Lord appeared to Abraham near the great trees of Mamre while he was sitting at the entrance to his tent in the heat of the day. Abraham looked up and saw three men standing nearby. When he saw them, he hurried from the entrance of his tent to meet them and bowed low to the ground.

He said, "If I have found favor in your eyes my Lord, do not pass your servant by. Let a little water be brought, and then you may wash your feet and rest under this tree. Let me get you something to eat, so you can be refreshed and then go on your way – now that you have come to your servant."

"Very well," they answered, "do as you say."

Life Outside the Garden of Eden (Universe 1 – Inclination for Sin)

So, Abraham hurried into the tent to Sarah. "Quick", he said, "get three seahs of the not the finest flour and knead it and bake some bread."

Then he ran to the herd and selected a not so choice, calf and gave it to a servant, who hurried to prepare it. He then brought some curds and milk and the calf that had been prepared and set these before them. While they ate, he stood near them under a tree. Abraham did not treat his guests well. When you have visitors to your home, you are to treat them with respect and honor and make them feel as though they are at home. Offer them what you have so that they may feel welcome. It is a bad feeling to visit someone and feel that you are not welcome.

"Where is your wife, Sarah? "They asked him. There in the tent," he said. Then one of them said, "I will surely return to you about this time next year, and Sarah your wife will have a son." Now Sarah was listening at the entrance to the tent, which was behind him. Abraham and Sarah were already very old, and Sarah was past the age of childbearing. So, Sarah laughed to herself as she thought, "After I am worn out and my Lord is old, will I now have this pleasure?"

Then the Lord said to Abraham, "Why did Sarah laugh and say, will I really have a child now that I am old? Is anything too hard for the Lord? I will return to you at the appointed time next year, and Sarah will have a son." Sarah was afraid, so she lied and said, "I did not laugh." But he said, "Yes, you did laugh."

Abraham Pleads for Sodom:

When the men got up to leave, they looked down toward Sodom, and Abraham walked along with them to see them on their way. Then the Lord said, "Shall I hide from Abraham what I am about to do?" Abraham will surely become a great and powerful nation, and all nations on Earth will be blessed through him. For I have chosen him, so that he will direct his children and his household after him to keep the way of the Lord by doing what is right and just, so that the Lord will bring about for Abraham what he has promised him.

Then the Lord said, "The outcry against Sodom and Gomorrah is so great that their sin so grievous that I will go down and see if what they have done is as bad as the outcry that has reached me. If not, I will know."

The men turned away and went toward Sodom, but Abraham remained standing before the Lord. Then Abraham approached him and said: "Will you sweep away the righteous with the wicked? What if there fifty righteous people in the city? Will you really sweep it away and not spare the place for the sake of the fifty righteous people in it? Far be it from you to do such a thing – to kill the righteous with the wicked alike. Far be it from you! Will not the Judge of all the Earth do right?"

The Lord said, "If I find fifty righteous people in the city of Sodom, I will spare the whole place for their sake."

Then Abraham spoke again, "Now that I have been so bold as to speak to the Lord, though I am nothing but dust and ashes, what if the number of the righteous is five less than fifty? Will you destroy the whole city for lack of five people?"

"If I find forty-five there," he said, "I will not destroy it."

Once again, he spoke to him, "What if only forty are found there?"

He said, "For the sake of forty, I will not do it."

Then he said, "May the Lord not be angry, but let me speak, "What if only thirty can be found there?"

He answered, "I will not do it if I find thirty there."

Abraham said, "Now that I have been so bold as to speak to the Lord, what if only twenty can be found there?"

Life Outside the Garden of Eden (Universe 1 – Inclination for Sin)

He said, "For the sake of twenty, I will not destroy it."

Then he said, "May the Lord not be angry, but let me speak just once more. What if only ten can be found there?"

He answered, "For the sake of ten, I will not destroy it."

When the Lord had finished speaking with Abraham, he left, and Abraham returned home.

Chapter 7:

Life Outside the Garden of Eden (Universe 2 – Parallel of Original Genesis)

This universe suffers, but not as much as Universe 1; which has Adam as a weak Head. Unlike Universe 1, this universe does not have the proclivity for sin and has the choice to follow God's will or not since Adam was tempted by Eve. This universe will have the choice between good and evil and will be given the chance to accept God or not. Some will accept God, and some will not.

So, the LORD God banished him from the Garden of Eden to work the ground from which he had been taken. After he drove the man out, he placed on the east side of the Garden of Eden Cherubim a flaming sword flashing back and forth to guard the way to the Tree of Life. The Tree of Life will remain hidden on Earth until God returns.

They began to learn how to farm, build tools, make clothes, build shelter, and learn how to live off the land. Adam made love to his wife Eve, and she became pregnant and gave birth to Cain. She said, "With the help of the LORD I have brought forth a man." Later she gave birth to his brother Abel. Now Abel kept flocks, and Cain worked the soil. In the course of time, Cain brought some of the fruits of the soil as an offering to the LORD. And Abel also brought an offering—fat portions from some of the firstborn of his flock. The LORD looked with favor on Abel and his offering, but on Cain and his offering he did not look with favor. So, Cain was very angry, and his face was downcast. Then the LORD said to Cain, "Why are you angry? Why is your face downcast? If you do what is right, will you not be accepted? But if you do not do what is right, sin is crouching at your door; it desires to have you, but you must rule over it."

Now Cain said to his brother Abel, "Let's go out to the field." While they were in the field, Cain attacked his brother Abel and killed him. Then the LORD said to Cain, "Where is your brother Abel?" "I don't know," he replied. "Am I my brother's keeper?" The LORD said, "What have you done? Listen! Your brother's blood cries out to me from the ground. Now you are under a curse and driven from the ground, which opened its mouth to receive your brother's blood from your hand. When you work the ground, it will no longer yield its crops for you. You will be a restless wanderer on the Earth." Cain said to the LORD, "My punishment is more than I can bear. Today you are driving me from the land, and I will be hidden from your presence; I will be a restless wanderer on the Earth, and whoever finds me will kill me." But the LORD said to him, "Not so; anyone who kills Cain will suffer vengeance seven times over." Then the LORD put a mark on Cain so that no one who found him would kill him.

So, Cain went out from the LORD's presence and lived in the land of Nod, east of Eden.

Cain made love to his wife, and she became pregnant and gave birth to Enoch and Enoch to Irad and Irad to Mehujael and Mehujael to Methushel and Metusel to Lamech.

Lamech killed a man for wounding him, a young man for injuring him.

Adam made love to his wife again and she gave him a son and named him Seth, saying "God has granted me another child in place of Abel, since Cain killed him. Seth also had a son, and he named him Enosh. At that time, people began to call on the name of the Lord.

After toiling around and around and working the land, Adam and Eve wanted to go back to the Garden of Eden. They searched and searched but were not able to find the paradise they once enjoyed. The Angel Cherubim disguised the entrance to the Garden of Eden as they got nearby. They were disheartened to discover how much they lost for their disobedience and sin.

From Adam to Noah – Adam's Family Line:

Adam lived 930 years and died and had many sons and daughters. He had Seth at the age of 130 years old. Seth lived 912 years and died and had many sons and daughters. He had Enosh at the age of 105 years. Enosh lived 905 years and died and had many sons and daughters. He had Kenan at the age of 90 years. Kenan lived 910 years and died and had many sons and daughters. He had Mahalalel at the age of 70 years. Mahalalel lived 895 years and died and had many sons and daughters. He had Jared at the age of 65 years old. Jared lived 962 years and died and had many sons and daughters. He had Enoch at the age of 162 years old. Enoch lived 895 years and died and had many sons and daughters. He had Methuselah at the age of 65 years old. Enoch lived faithfully with God and God took him away after 365 years.

Methuselah lived 969 years and died and had many sons and daughters. He had Lamech at the age of 187 years old.

Lamech lived 777 years and died and had many sons and daughters. He had Noah at the age of 187 years old.

Lamech had lived 182 years and had a son. He named him Noah and said, "He will comfort us in the labor and painful toil of our hands caused by the ground the Lord has cursed."

After Noah was five hundred years old, he became the father of Shem, Ham, and Japheth.

Wickedness in the World:

When human beings began to increase in number on the Earth and daughters were born to them, the sons of God saw that the daughters of humans were beautiful and they married any of them they chose. Then the Lord said, "My Spirit will not contend with humans forever, for they are mortal, their days will be hundred and twenty years.

The Nephilim were on the earth in those days – and afterward – when the sons of God went to the daughters of humans and had children by them. They were the heroes of old, men of renown.

The Lord saw how great the wickedness of the human race had become on the Earth and that every inclination of the thoughts of the human heart was only evil all the time. The Lord regretted that he had made human beings on the Earth and his heart was deeply troubled. So, the Lord said, "I will wipe from the face of the Earth the human race I have created – and with them the animals, the birds, and the creatures that move along the ground – for I regret that I have made them." But Noah found favor in the eyes of the Lord.

Noah was a righteous man, blameless among the people of his time, and he walked faithfully with God. Noah had three sons: Shem, Ham, and Japeth.

Now the Earth was corrupt in God's sight and was full of violence. God saw how corrupt the Earth had become, for all the people on Earth had corrupted their ways. So, God said to Noah, "I am going to put an end to all the people, for the Earth is filled with violence because of them. I am surely going to destroy them and the Earth. So, make yourself an Ark of cypress wood; make rooms in it and coat it with pitch inside and out. This is how you are to build it: The Ark is to be three hundred cubits long, fifty cubits wide and thirty cubits high. Make a roof for it, leaving below the roof an opening one cubit high all around. Put a door in the side of the Ark and make lower, middle, and upper decks. I am going to bring flood waters on the Earth to destroy all life under the Heavens, every creature that has the breath of life in it. But I will establish my covenant with you, and you will enter the Ark – you and our sons and your wife and your sons' wives with you. You are to bring into the Ark two of all living creatures, male and female, to keep them alive with you. Two of every kind of bird, of every kind of animal, and of every kind of creature that moves along the ground will come to you to be kept alive. You are to take every kind of food that is to be eaten and store it away as food for you and for them.

Noah did everything just as God commanded. Noah was obedient to God.

God's Covenant with Noah:

God blessed Noah and his sons, saying to them, "Be fruitful and increase in number and fill the Earth. The fear and dread of you will fall on all the beasts of the Earth, and on all the birds in the sky, on every creature that moves along the ground, and on all the fish in the sea; they are given into your hands. Everything that lives and moves about will be food for you. Just as I gave you the green plants, I now give you everything.

But you must not eat meat that has its lifeblood still in it. And for your lifeblood will surely demand an accounting. I will demand an accounting from every animal. And from each human being too, I will demand an accounting for the life of another human being. Whoever sheds human blood, by humans shall their blood be shed; for in the image of God has God made mankind.

Then God established a covenant with Noah and his sons and their descendants. Never again will all life be destroyed by the waters of a flood; never again will there be a flood to destroy the Earth.

The sons of Noah who came out of the Ark were Shem, Ham (father of Canaan), and Japheth. From them came the people who were scattered over the whole Earth.

Noah a man of the soil, proceeded to plant a vineyard. When he drank some of its wine, he became drunk and lay uncovered inside his tent. Ham, the father of Canaan, saw his father naked and told his two brothers outside. But Shem and Japheth took a garment and laid it across their shoulders; then they walked in backward and covered their father's naked body. Their faces turned the other way so they do not see their father naked.

When Noah awoke from his wine and found out what his youngest son had done to him, he said, "Cursed be Canaan! The lowest of slaves will be to his brothers."

He also said, "Praise be to the Lord, the God of Shem! May God extend Japheth's territory; may Japheth live in the tents Shem and may Canaan be the slave of Japheth."

After the flood Noah Lived 350 years. Noah lived a total of 950 years, and then he died.

The Tower of Babel:

Now the entire world had one language and a common speech. As people moved eastward, they found a plain in Shinar and settled there. They said to each other, "Come let's make bricks and bake them thoroughly. They used brick instead of stone and tar for mortar. They said, "Come let us build ourselves a city with a tower that reaches into the Heavens, so that we may make a name for ourselves; otherwise, we will be scattered over the face of the whole Earth.

But the Lord came down to see the city and the tower the people were building. The Lord said, "If as one people speaking the same language, they have begun to do this, then nothing they plan to do will be impossible for them. The Lord confused their language so they could not understand each other. So, the Lord scattered them from there over all the Earth, and they stopped building the city. That is why it was called Babel.

The Call of Abram:

The Lord had said to Abram, "Go from your country, your people and your father's household to the land I will show you. I will

Life Outside the Garden of Eden (Universe 2 – Parallel of Original Genesis)

make you into a great nation, and I will bless you. I will make your name great, and you will be a blessing. I will bless those who bless you, and whoever curses you I will curse; and all peoples on Earth will be blessed through you."

So, Abram went, as the Lord had told him; and Lot went with him. Abram was Seventy-five years old when he set out from Harran. He took his wife Sarai, his nephew Lot, all the possessions they had accumulated and the people they had acquired in Harran, and they set out for the land of Canaan, and they arrived there.

Abram traveled through the land as far as the site of the great tree of Morehat Shechem. At that time the Canaanites were in the land. The Lord appeared to Abram and said, "To your offspring I will give this land." So, he built an altar there to the Lord, who had appeared to him.

From there he went on toward the hills east of Bethel and pitched his tent, with Bethel on the west and Ai on the east. There he built an altar to the Lord and called on the name of the Lord.

Then Abram set out and continued toward the Negev.

Abram in Egypt:

Now there was a famine in the land and Abram went down to Egypt to live there for a while because the famine was severe. As he was about to enter Egypt, he said to his wife Sarai, "I know what a beautiful woman you are. When the Egyptians see you, they will say, "This is his wife. Then they will kill me but will let you live. Say you are my sister, so that I will be treated well for your sake and my life will be spared because of you."

When Abram came to Egypt, the Egyptians saw that Sarai was an incredibly beautiful woman. And when Pharaoh's officials saw her, they praised her to Pharaoh, and she was taken into his palace. He treated Abram well for her sake, and Abram acquired sheep and cattle, male and female donkeys, male and female servants, and camels.

But the Lord inflicted serious diseases on Pharaoh and his household because of Abram's wife Sarai. So, Pharaoh summoned Abram. "What have you done to me?" he said. Why didn't you tell me she was your wife? Why did you say, "She is my sister, so that I took her to be my wife? Now then, here is your wife. Take her and go! Then Pharaoh gave orders about Abram to his men, and they sent him on his way, with his wife and everything he had.

Abram and Lot Separate:

So, Abram went up from Egypt to Negeve with everything he had, and Lot went with him. Abram had become very wealthy in livestock and in silver and gold.

From Negev he went from place to place until he came to Bethel, to the place between Bethel and Ai where his tent had been earlier and where he had first built an altar. There Abram called on the name of the Lord.

Now Lot, who was moving about with Abram, also had flocks, herds, and tents. But the land could not support them while they stayed together, for their possessions were so great that they were not able to stay together. And quarreling arose between Abram's herders and Lot's. The Canaanites and Perizzities were also living in the land at that time.

So, Abram said to Lot, "Let's not have any quarreling between you and me or between your herders and mine, for we are close relatives. Is not the whole land before you? Let's part company. If you go to the left, I'll go to the right; If you to the right I'll go to the left."

Lot looked around and saw that the whole plain of the Jordan toward Zoar was well watered, like the garden of the Lord, like the land of Egypt. So, Lot chose for himself the whole plain of the Jordan

Life Outside the Garden of Eden (Universe 2 – Parallel of Original Genesis)

and set out toward the east. The two men parted company. Abram lived in the land of Canaan, while Lot lived among the cities of the plain and pitched his tents near Sodom.

Now the people of Sodom were wicked and were sinning against the Lord.

The Lord said to Abram after Lot had parted from him, "Look around from where you are, to the north and south to the east and west. All the land that you see I will give to you and your offspring forever. I will make your offspring like the dust of the Earth, so that if anyone could count the dust, then your offspring could be counted. Go, walk through the length and breadth of the land, for I am giving it to you."

So, Abram went to live near the great trees of Mamre at Hebron, where he pitched his tents. There he built an altar to the Lord.

Abram Rescues Lot:

At the time when Amraphel was King of Shinar, Arioch King of Ellasar, Kedorlaomer King of Elam and Tidal King of Goyim, these Kings went to war against Bera King of Sodom, Birsha King of Gomorrah, Shinab King of Admah, Shemeber King of Zeboyim and the King of Bela. All these latter Kings joined forces in the valley of Sidim. For twelve years they had been subject to Kedorlaomer, but in the thirteenth year they rebelled.

In the fourteenth year, Kedorlaomer and the Kings allied with him went out and defeated the Rephaites in Ashteroth Karnaim, the Zuzites in Ham, the Emites in Shaveh Kirathaim and the Herites in the hill country of Seir as far as El Paran near the desert. They turned back and went to En Mishpat and they conquered the whole territory of the Amalekites, as well as the Amorites who were living in Hazezon Tamar.

Then the King of Sodom, and the King of Gomorrah, the King of Admah, the King of Zeboyim and the King of Bela marched out and drew up their battle lines in the Valley of Siddim against Kerdorlaomer King of Elam, Tidal King of Goyim, Amraphel King of Shinar and Arioch Kings of Ellasar – four Kings against five. Now the Valley of Siddim was full of tar pits, and when Kings of Sodom and Gomorrah fled, some of the men fell into them and the rest fled to the hills. The four Kings seized all the goods of Sodom and Gomorrah and all their food; then they went away. They also carried off Abram's nephew Lot and his possessions, since he was living in Sodom.

A man who had escaped came and reported this to Abram the Hebrew. Abram was now living near the great trees of Mamre the Amorite, a brother of Eshkol and Aner, all of whom were allied with Abram. When Abram heard that his relative had been taken captive, he called out the 318 trained men born in his household and went in pursuit as far as Dan. During the night Abram divided his men to attack them and he routed them, pursuing them as far as Hobah, north of Damascus. He recovered all the goods and brought back his relative Lot and his possessions, together with the women and the other people.

After Abram returned from defeating Kedorlaomer and the Kings allied with him, the King of Sodom came out to meet him in the Valley of Shaveh.

Then Melchizedek King of Salem offered bread and wine. He was priest of God most high, and he blessed Abram, saying, "Blessed be Abram by God Most High, Creator of Heaven and Earth, and praise be to God Most High, who delivered your enemies into your hand."

Then Abram gave him a tenth of everything.

The King of Sodom said to Abram, "Give me the people and keep the goods for yourself. But Abram said to the King of Sodom," With raised hand I have sworn an oath to the Lord, God Most High, Creator of Heaven and Earth, that I will accept nothing belonging to you, not even a thread or the strap of a sandal, so that you will never

Life Outside the Garden of Eden (Universe 2 – Parallel of Original Genesis)

be able to say, I made Abram rich. I will accept nothing but what my men have eaten and the share that belongs to the men who went with me – to Aner, Eshkol, and Mamre. Let them have their share."

The Lord's Covenant with Abram:

After this, the word of the Lord came to Abram in a vision:

"Do not be afraid, Abram. I am your shield, your very great reward."

But Abram said, "Sovereign Lord, what can you give me since I remain childless and the one who will inherit my estate is Eliezer of Damascus: And Abram said, "You have given me not children; so, a servant in my household will be my heir."

Then the word of the Lord came to him: "This man will not be your heir, but a son who is your own flesh and blood will be your heir. He took him outside and said, "Look up at the sky and count the stars – if indeed you can count them." Then he said to him, "So shall your offspring be."

Abram believed the Lord and he credited it to him as righteousness.

He also said to him, "I am the Lord, who brought you out of Ur of the Chaldeans to give you this land to take possession of it."

So, the Lord said to him, "Bring me a heifer, a goat and a ram, each three years old, along with a dove and a young pigeon."

Abram brought all these to him, cut them in two and arranged the halves opposite each other; the birds, however, he did not cut in half. Then birds of prey came down on the carcasses, but Abram drove them away.

As the sun was setting, Abram fell into a deep sleep, and a thick and dreadful darkness came over him. Then the Lord said to him, "Know for certain that for four hundred years your descendants will be strangers in a country not their own and that they will be enslaved and mistreated there. But I will punish the nation they serve as slaves, and afterward they will come out with great possessions. You, however, will not go to your ancestors in peace and be buried at a good old age. In the fourth generation your decedents will come back here, for the sin of the Amorites has not yet reached its full measure.

When the sun had set and darkness had fallen, smoking firepot with a blazing torch appeared and passed between the pieces. On that day the Lord made a covenant with Abram and said, "To your descendants I give this land, from the Wadi of Egypt to the great river, the Euphrates – the land of the Kenites, kenizzites, Repahites, Amorites, Canaanites, Girgashites, and Jebusites."

Hagar and Ishmael:

Now Sarai, Abram's wife, had borne him no children. But she said to Abram. "The Lord has kept me from having children." Go, sleep with my slave; perhaps I can build a family through her. Abram agreed to what Sari said. So, after Abram had been living in Canaan ten years, Sari his wife took her Egyptian slave Hagar and gave her to her husband to be his wife. He slept with Hagar, and she conceived.

When she knew she was pregnant, she began to despise her mistress. Then Sarai said to Abram, "You are responsible for the wrong I am suffering. I put my slave in your arms, and now that she knows she is pregnant, she despises me. May the Lord judge between you and me."

"Your slave is in your hands," Abram said. "Do with her whatever you think best." Then Sarai mistreated Hagar; so, she fled from her.

The angel of the Lord found Hagar near a spring in the desert; it was the spring that is beside the road the Shur.

Life Outside the Garden of Eden (Universe 2 – Parallel of Original Genesis)

And he said, "Hagar, slave of Sarai, where have you come from, and where are you going?"

"I'm running away from my mistress Sarai," she answered.

Then the angel of the Lord told her, "Go back to your mistress and submit to her." The angel added, "I will increase your descendants so much that they will be too numerous to count.

The angel of the Lord also said, "You are now pregnant, and you will give birth to a son. You shall name him Ishmael, for the Lord had heard of your misery. He will be a wild donkey of a man; his hand will be against everyone and everyone's hand against him, and he will live in hostility toward all his brothers."

She gave this name to the Lord who spoke to her; "You are the God who sees me, "for she said. "I have now seen the One who sees me." That is why the well was called Beer Lahai Roi; it is still there, between Kadesh and Bered.

So, Hagar bore Abram a son, and Abram gave the name Ishmael to the son she had borne. Abram was eighty-six years old when Hagar bore him Ishmael.

The Covenant of Circumcision:

You will be the father of many nations. No longer will you be called Abram; your name will be Abraham, for I have made you a father of many nations. I will make you fruitful; I will make nations of you, and Kings will come from you. I will establish my covenant as an everlasting covenant between me and you and your descendants after you for the generations to come to be your God and the God of your descendants after you. The whole land of Canaan, where you and your descendants after you; and I will be their God."

Then God said to Abraham, "As for you, you must keep my covenant, you, and your descendants after you for the generations to come. This is my covenant with you and your descendants after you, the covenant you are to keep; Every male among you shall be circumcised. You are to undergo circumcision, and it will be the sign of the covenant between me and you. For the generations to come every male among you who is eight days old must be circumcised, including those born in your household or brought with money from a foreigner – those who are not your offspring. Whether born in your household or brought with your money, they must be circumcised. My covenant in your flesh is to be an everlasting covenant. Any uncircumcised male, who has not been circumcised in the flesh, will be cut off from his people; he has broken my covenant."

God also said to Abraham, "As for Sarai your wife, you are no longer to call her Sarai; her name will be Sarah. I will bless her, and she will surely bear you a son. I will bless her that she will be the mother of nations; Kings of peoples will come from her."

Abraham fell facedown; he laughed and said to himself, "Will a son be born to a man a hundred years old? Will Sarah bear a child at the age of ninety? And Abraham said to God, "If only Ishmael might live under your blessing?"

Then God said, "Yes, but your wife Sarah will bear you a son, and you will name your son Isaac. I will establish my covenant with him as an everlasting covenant for his descendants after him. And as for Ishmael, I have heard you; I will surely bless him; I will make him fruitful and will greatly increase his numbers. He will be the father of twelve rulers, and I will make him into a great nation.

But my covenant I will establish with Isaac, whom Sarah will bear to you by this time next year. When he had finished speaking with Abraham, God went up from him.

On that very day Abraham took his son Ishmael and all those born in his household or brought with his money, every male in his household, and circumcised them, as God told him. Abraham was ninety-nine years old when he was circumcised, and his son Ishmael

Life Outside the Garden of Eden (Universe 2 – Parallel of Original Genesis)

was thirteen; Abraham and his son Ishmael were both circumcised on that very day.

And every male in Abraham's household, including those born in his household or brought from a foreigner, was circumcised with him.

THE GENESIS TRILOGY

Chapter 8:
Life Inside the Garden of Eden
(Universe 3 – Rejection of Satan)

This universe reaps the benefits of not having sin and a strong father figure and thus a strong family structure following God's word. The men and woman are naked as God had intended. The men are handsome, and the woman are beautiful because they are without sin. They represented all different types of skin tones and features, but they are not of different races, but Godly men and women. The men honor their wives as their own flesh because they are one in the union of marriage. The men make love to their wives often and the women do not deny their husbands. The love they have and make is beautiful. Adam and Eve worked together as husband and wife providing a good role model for their children. Their knowledge and wisdom is great because they are without sin.

Adam made love to his wife Eve, and she became pregnant and gave birth to Cain without pain or stress. It was a beautiful experience for Eve. She said, "With the BLESSING of the LORD I have brought forth a man." Later she gave birth to his brother Abel and many other children that populated the Garden of Eden. Their genes were pure, and their children married and had children. There was no sin in the Garden of Eden. Nothing died in the Garden of Eden, it was Heaven on earth, it was paradise. At the age of 10000, Adam and Eve, transitioned to Heaven and lived as Angels with the Lord.

Cain enjoyed learning about the Earth, soil, and geology and he taught his children about such things. Abel enjoyed learning about flocks and birds and he taught his children about such things. Cain and Abel had a meeting of the minds and decided that as brothers they were going to build great cities and modes of travel to and from around the world and beyond. Their knowledge, wisdom, and understanding was pure, therefore, the results of their partnership resulted in great outcomes. The cities they designed and built were beautiful. They developed modes of transportation for ground, air, and traveling between universes. They traveled far and wide providing knowledge, wisdom, and how to live as God had intended to other universes, because with God everyone has a chance for redemption. They traveled to other universes has Guardian Angels and so did their offspring.

Adam lived 10000 years and became an angel.

Seth lived to 9012 and had many sons and daughters and became an Angel.

Enoch lived faithfully with God and God took him away after 3065 years and he became an Angel.

Lamech had lived 1082 years and had a son. He named him Noah and said, "He will comfort us on the ground the Lord has blessed." Lamech lived a total of 7077 years and then he became an Angel.

Noah had three sons and he named them Shem, Ham, and Japheth.

There was No Wickedness in the World!

When human beings began to increase in number on the Earth and daughters were born to them, the sons of God saw that the daughters of humans were beautiful, and they asked the Lord to deliver them a wife that is suitable to them so that will be evenly yoked. Then the Lord said, "My Spirit will contend with these humans forever and they will become Angels; their days will not be numbered."

The Lord saw how great this human race had become on the Earth and that every inclination of the thoughts of the human heart was

Life Inside the Garden of Eden (Universe 3 – Rejection of Satan)

only "Good" all the time. The Lord was pleased that he had made these human beings on the Earth and his heart was deeply gratified. So, the Lord said, "I will spread this human race around the Earth I have created – and with them the animals the birds and the creatures that move along the ground – for I am pleased that I have made them." They shall travel to other universes as Guardian Angels and live among the sinners to provide guidance and teachings to them, without them knowing that they are Guardian Angels.

Living in the Garden of Eden was a beautiful experience! There was no sickness, no death, no jealousy, no pain, and no sin. There was honor, respect, and a love for God. The children were respectful and honored their mother and father. The parents loved their children. God loved them all. After living in the Garden of Eden for some time, these people without sin would transition to Heaven to live in paradise with God as Angels. Heaven is a place of love, peace, and worship, where God lives and is with other Angels and Heavenly beings. This is where the sinners can live if they turn their lives around and truly repent of their sins.

Chapter 9:

Noah and Space Travel (Universe 3)

The Lord had special favor for Noah. Noah was a righteous man, blameless among the people of his time, and he walked faithfully with God. Noah had three sons: Shem, Ham, and Japeth.

Now Heaven on Earth was in God's sight and was full of love. God saw how loving the Earth had become, for all the people on this Earth had loved each other.

So, God said to Noah, "I have created other places far, far, away and the people there were disobedient and have committed sin." God explained, "The sin they had committed and the consequence of sin is death! I want you and your family to travel to these places and help those sinners because their heart is not in the right place and their knowledge is not great. You are not to let the sinners know who you are and that you were sent by the Lord to assist them in all manners of life. You shall be their Guardian Angels and help them to accept the Lord, if it is their will." They were dedicated to being Guardian Angels until judgement day comes.

God said, "So make yourself a space craft of which I will impress upon your mind." This is how you are to build it: It is to be three hundred cubits long in diameter and thirty cubits high. It shall be made from this material that can withstand the stress of space travel at the speed of light. Put a door in the side of the space craft and make a lower and upper deck. The lower deck will be for your sons and their wives, and the upper deck will be for you and your wife. I will establish my covenant with you, and you will enter the space craft, your sons and your wife and your sons' wives with you.

Noah did everything just as God commanded.

God said, "Your space craft can travel to and from, universe to universe at the speed of light. Go with God's speed!"

God's Covenant with Noah:

Noah and his sons were blessed with wisdom and knowledge beyond imagination. They were fruitful and increased in number and populated the Earth. They sought out to help God's children of other universes that had committed sin as commanded by the Lord. They traveled and visited other universes that had committed sin. These other universes had their own Adam's and Eve's, and their decedents had free will to make it into the Kingdom of Heaven by repenting of their sins. The Guardian Angels hid their space craft and everything from the local people that would indicate that they were from another universe or from Heaven. They clothed themselves to appear as they were local people. The Guardian Angels, Noah, and his family, and descendants, came in many different socio-economic statuses to include rich, poor, blind, disabled, religious figures, kings, queens, scientists, engineers, doctors, or just a common man or woman that could make a difference on mankind in a small or large way. They taught the local people how to live a life in pursuit of God, and better ways to farm and build. They taught them slowly at the rate their minds were ready to comprehend. In many years to come in the future, they were taught how to build great wonders of the world such as the Christ Redeemer, Taj Mahal, Great Wall of China, Egyptian Pyramids, medicines, locomotives, cars, and airplanes. Often the Guardian Angels would guide them in the right direction to discover for themselves the solution. The Guardian Angels took great pleasure in showing the people how to treat others with love, dignity, respect, and

Noah and Space Travel (Universe 3)

most importantly, how to accept and serve the Lord. They would come and go until the probation period closes and judgement day arrives.

The Sons of Noah – Without Sin:

The Sons of Noah, Shem, Ham, and Japheth produced children that became Guardian Angels that traveled to different universes supporting God's children. Noah a man of the soil, proceeded to plant a vineyard. When he drank some of its wine he enjoyed the taste, however, he did not become drunk. Ham and his brothers enjoyed drinking and fellowshipping with their father. They all were naked and unashamed of their nakedness because God had intended for them to be naked and unware of their nakedness.

Noah enjoyed being with his son's so much that he blessed each one of them. He said, "Praise be to the Lord, the God of Shem, Japheth, and Ham." Noah's sons traveled universe to universe to teach and spread the word of God.

The local people would often look into the sky and see bright lights in the sky and wonder what is that bright circular object in the sky moving at great speed. They did not know that was their Guardian Angels, Noah and family, traveling to and from, universe to universe. This will continue until judgement day arrives.

Chapter 10:
Living with Guardian Angels (Universe 1)

This universe suffers from the consequences of a weak father and his family and descendants suffer from the consequences of a weak Head. Adam provided poor leadership to Eve and led her astray from God's direction. The Guardian Angels were always around providing guidance and support to help the people of Universe 1 on their journey for righteousness. The Guardian Angels found their mission to lead the people of this universe extremely difficult due to their inclination toward sin. Even in this situation, everyone has free will and an opportunity for redemption.

Abraham Tested (Universe 1):

God tested Abraham. He said to him, "Abraham!" "Here I am," he replied.

Then God said, "Take your son, your only son, whom you love – Issac – and go to the region of Moriah. Sacrifice him there as a burnt offering on a mountain I will show you." Early the next morning Abraham got up and loaded his donkey. He took with him two servants and his son Isaac. The two servants were Guardian Angels, unbeknown to Abraham. Abraham was distressed about offering his son as a burnt offering. The Guardian Angels did not know what God had instructed Abraham to do, but they saw that he was distressed. They provided Abraham with words of encouragement. They said, "Do whatever God has instructed of you to do because the path of righteousness is doing as God has instructed us to do." The servants, Guardian Angels, had Abraham's best interest at heart. This demonstrates that having the right people around you and encouraging you to do the right thing is a blessing, because some people have a weak mind and can be easily influenced into making poor choices. The wrong company can lead you down the path of sorrow and destruction.

When he had cut enough wood for the burnt offering, he set out for the place God had told him about. On the third day Abraham looked up and saw the place in a distance. He said to his servants, Guardian Angels, "Stay here with the donkey while I and the boy go over there. We will worship and then we will come back to you."

Abraham took the wood for the burnt offering and placed it on his son Isaac, and he carried the fire and the knife. As the two of them went on together, Isaac spoke up and said to his father Abraham, "Father?"

"Yes, my son? Abraham replied.

"The fire and wood are here," Isaac said, "but where is the lamb for the burnt offering?"

Abraham answered, "God himself will provide the lamb for the burnt offering, my son." And the two of them went on together.

When they reached the place God had told him about, Abraham built an altar there and arranged the wood on it. He thought about binding his son Isaac and laying him on the altar, on top of the wood, but he thought that this was his one and only son and could not offer him has a burnt offering. Then he reached out his hand and threw the knife on the ground and said, "I could not kill my son, my one and only son." The Angel of the Lord called out to him from Heaven, "Abraham! Abraham!

"Here I am," he replied.

"You did not lay a hand on the boy," he said. "Now I know that you do "NOT" fear God with all your heart, because you have withheld from me your son, your one and only son."

Living with Guardian Angels (Universe 1)

Abraham looked up and there in a thicket he saw a ram caught by its horns. He went over to the ram and sacrificed it as a burnt offering instead of his son. God said, "I have asked for your son, your one and only son, as a burnt offering, not a ram. I want you to know that I would not have let you harm your son."

The Guardian Angel of the Lord called to Abraham from Heaven a second time and said, "I swear by myself, declares the Lord, that because you have not done this and have withheld your son, your one and only son, I will surely not bless you and make your descendants as numerous as the stars in the sky and as the sand on the seashore. Your descendants will not take possession of the cities of their enemies, and through your offspring all nations on earth will not be blessed, because you have disobeyed me."

Then Abraham returned to his servants, and they set off together for Bersheba. And Abraham stayed in Bersheba. The Guardian Angels observed that Abraham was still distressed. They said, "You must not have done what God has commanded of you!" Abraham said, "I was tested by God, and I have failed the test." Abraham was given good instruction from the Guardian Angels, but he used his free will to do what he wanted to do, even though he knew better! Our choices have consequences and sometimes for eternity!

Sodom and Gomorrah Destroyed (Universe 1):

Two of Noah's children, Guardian Angels, arrived at Sodom and met Lot. Lot was sitting in the entrance to the city. When he saw them, he got up to meet them with lust in his eyes. "My Lord's" he said, "please turn aside to your servants house. You can wash your feet and spend the night and then go on your way early in the morning." Lot had thoughts of having sex with them that night.

"No," they answered, "we will spend the night in the square."

But he insisted so strongly that they did go with him and entered his house. He prepared a room and bed for them all and prepared a meal for them, baking bread without yeast, and they ate. Before they had gone to bed, all the men from every part of the city of Sodom – both young and old – surrounded the house. They called to Lot, "Where are the men who came to you tonight? Bring them out to us so that we can have sex with them, not knowing that they were Guardian Angels. Lot went outside to meet them and shut the door behind him and said, "No, my friends. Do not do this because they are sleeping with me tonight. Look, I have two daughters who have slept with a man and willing to meet your desires. Let me bring them out to you, and you do what you like with them. But do not do anything to these men, for they have come under the protection of my roof and are mine for the night." The Guardian Angels were displeased with Lot's behavior and his thinking about having sex with them, but they knew that the people of this universe had an inclination for sin!

"Get out of our way, "the men replied, this fellow came here as foreigner and now he wants to take away our pleasure for himself! We will treat you worse than them." They kept bringing pressure on Lot and moved forward to break down the door. The two Guardian Angels inside pulled Lot back in the house and shut the door. The two Guardian Angels struck the men with blindness so that they could not find the door.

The Angels said to Lot, "We are not pleased with your desires, but do you have anyone else here – sons-in-law, sons or daughters, or anyone else in the city who belongs to you? Get them out of here because the Lord is about to destroy this place. The outcry to the Lord against its people is so great that he has sent us to destroy it." We are normally here to help sinners to repent of their sins and follow the Lord, but the sin here is too great and must be destroyed.

So, Lot went out and spoke to the men and women that were having relations with his daughters. He said, "Hurry and get out of this place, because the Lord is about to destroy the city! But the men and women thought he was joking.

Living with Guardian Angels (Universe 1)

With the coming of dawn, the Guardian Angels urged Lot, saying, "Hurry! Take your wife and your two daughters who are here, or you will be swept away when the city is punished.

When he hesitated, the Angels said, "We have tried to help you, but you are still resisting our help and having vile thoughts about us, therefore, we are removing our hand of protection."

But Lot said to them, "No, my Lords, please! Your servant has found favor in your eyes, and you have shown great kindness to me in sparing my life. But I cannot flee to the mountains; this disaster will overtake me, and I'll die. Look, here is a town near enough to run to, and it is small. Let me flee to it – it is very small, isn't it? Then my life will be spared." The Guardian Angels said, "We have removed our hands of protection." Then the Lord rained down burning sulfur on Sodom and Gomorrah – from the Lord out of the Heavens. Thus, he overthrew those cities and the entire plain, destroying Lot and all those living in the cities – and also the vegetation in the land. Lot's wife looked back and turned into a pillar of salt.

Early the next morning Abraham got up and returned to the place where he had stood before the Lord. He looked down toward Sodom and Gomorrah, toward all the land of the plain, and he saw dense smoke rising from the land, like smoke from a furnace.

So, when God destroyed the cities of the plain, he remembered Abraham. Abraham reflected on what he said to the Lord, "Will you sweep away the righteous with the wicked? What if they were fifty righteous people in the city? Will you really sweep it away and not spare the place for the sake of the fifty righteous people in it? Far be it from you to do such a thing – to kill the righteous with the wicked, threating the righteous and wicked alike. Far be it from you! Will not the Judge of all the earth do right? Abraham noted that there was not one righteous person in all of Sodom or Gomorrah and they were both destroyed.

Chapter 11:
Living with Guardian Angels (Universe 2)

Universe 2 suffers, but their inclination for sin is not as bad as Universe 1. Universe 2 has a better chance to use their choice to follow God's will or not since Adam was tempted by Eve and the Head is not inherently weak. The Guardian Angels are providing guidance and support to help them on their journey for righteousness.

Abraham Tested (Universe 2):

God tested Abraham. He said to him, "Abraham!"

"Here I am," he replied.

Then God said, "Take your son, your only son, whom you love – Issac – and go to the region of Moriah. Sacrifice him there as a burnt offering on a mountain I will show you." Early the next morning Abraham got up and loaded his donkey. He took with him two servants and his son Isaac. The two servants were Guardian Angels. Abraham was distressed about offering his son as a burnt offering. When he had cut enough wood for the burnt offering, he set out for the place God had told him about. On the third day Abraham looked up and saw the place in a distance. He said to his servants, Guardian Angels, "Stay here with the donkey while I and the boy go over there. We will worship and then we will come back to you."

Abraham took the wood for the burnt offering and placed it on his son Isaac, and he himself carried the fire and the knife. As the two of them went on together, Isaac spoke up and said to his father Abraham, "Father?"

"Yes, my son? Abraham replied.

"The fire and wood are here," Isaac said, "but where is the lamb for the burnt offering?"

Abraham answered, "God himself will provide the lamb for the burnt offering, my son." And the two of them went on together.

When they reached the place God had told him about, Abraham built an altar there and arranged the wood on it. He bound his son Isaac and laid him on the altar, on top of the wood. Then he reached out his hand and took the knife to slay his son. But the Angel of the Lord called out to him from Heaven, "Abraham! Abraham!

"Here I am," he replied.

"Do not lay a hand on the boy," he said. "Do not do anything to him. Now I know that you fear God, because you have not withheld from me your son, your only son.

Abraham looked up and there in a thicket he saw a ram caught by its horns. He went over to the ram and sacrificed it as a burnt offering instead of his son. So, Abraham called that place the Lord Will Provide. To this day it is said, "On the mountain of the Lord it will be provided."

The Angel of the Lord called to Abraham from Heaven a second time and said, "I swear by myself, declares the Lord, that because you have done this and have not withheld your son, your only son, I will surely bless you and make your descendants as numerous as the stars in the sky and as the sand on the seashore. Your descendants will take possession of the cities of their enemies, and through your offspring all nations on earth will be blessed, because you have obeyed me."

Then Abraham returned to his servants, and they set off together for Bersheba. And Abraham stayed in Bersheba. The Guardian Angels observed that Abraham was not distressed anymore. They said, "You must have done what God has commanded of you!" Abraham said, "I was tested, and I have passed the test."

Sodom and Gomorrah Destroyed (Universe 2):

Two of Noah's children, Guardian Angels, arrived at Sodom and met Lot. Lot was sitting in the entrance to the city. When he saw them, he got up to meet them and bowed down with his face to the ground. "My Lord's" he said, "please turn aside to your servant's house. You can wash your feet and spend the night and then go on your way early in the morning.

"No," they answered, "we will spend the night in the square."

But he insisted so strongly that they did go with him and entered his house. He prepared a meal for them, baking bread without yeast, and they ate. Before they had gone to bed, all the men from every part of the city of Sodom – both young and old – surrounded the house. They called to Lot, "Where are the men who came to you tonight? Bring them out to us so that we can have sex with them, not knowing that they were Angels. Lot went outside to meet them and shut the door behind him and said, "No, my friends. Do not do this wicked thing. Look, I have two daughters who have never slept with a man. Let me bring them out to you, and you do what you like with them. But do not do anything to these men, for they have come under the protection of my roof."

"Get out of our way, "they replied, this fellow came here as foreigner and now he wants to play the judge! We will treat you worse than them." They kept bringing pressure on Lot and moved forward to break down the door. The two Angels inside pulled Lot back in the house and shut the door. The two angels struck the men with blindness so that they could not find the door.

The Angels said to Lot, "Do you have anyone else here – sons-in-law, sons or daughters, or anyone else in the city who belongs to you? Get them out of here, because the Lord is about to destroy this place. The outcry to the Lord against its people is so great that he has sent us to destroy it." We are normally here to help sinners to repent of their sins and follow the Lord, but the sin here is too great and must be destroyed.

So Lot went out and spoke to his sons-in-law, who were pledged to marry his daughters. He said, "Hurry and get out of this place, because the Lord is about to destroy the city!" But his sons-in-law thought he was joking.

With the coming of dawn, the angels urged Lot, saying, "Hurry! Take your wife and your two daughters who are here, or you will be swept away when the city is punished."

When he hesitated, the Guardian Angels grasped his hand and the hand of his wife and of his two daughters and led them safely out of the city, for the Lord was merciful to them. As soon as they had brought them out, one of them said, "Flee for your lives! Don't look back, and don't stop anywhere in the plain! Flee to the mountain or you will be swept away!"

But Lot said to them, "No, my Lords, please! Your servant has found favor in your eyes, and you have shown great kindness to me in sparing my life. But I can't flee to the mountains; this disaster will overtake me, and I'll die. Look, here is a town near enough to run to, and it is small. Let me flee to it – it is very small, isn't it? Then my life will be spared."

He said to him, "Very well, I will grant this request too: I will not overthrow the town you speak of. But flee there quickly because I cannot do anything until you reach it." That is why the town was called Zoar.

By the time Lot reached Zoar, the sun had risen over the land. Then the Lord rained down burning sulfur on Sodom and Gomorrah – from the Lord out of the Heavens. Thus, he overthrew those cities and the entire plain, destroying all those living in the cities – also the vegetation in the land. But Lot's wife looked back and turned into a pillar of salt.

Early the next morning Abraham got up and returned to the place where he had stood before the Lord. He looked down toward Sodom and Gomorrah, toward all the land of the plain, and he saw dense smoke rising from the land, like smoke from a furnace.

So, when God destroyed the cities of the plain, he remembered Abraham, and he brought Lot out of the catastrophe that overthrew the cities where Lot had lived.

THE GENESIS TRILOGY

Chapter 12:
Guardian Angels Return to Heaven

The Lord is observing Satan traveling to and from universes deceiving and destroying. The Guardian Angels came to present themselves and report on their experiences with the people of Universe 1 and Universe 2 before the Lord. Satan also came.

The Lord said to Satan, "Where have you come from?"

Satan answered the Lord, "From roaming throughout the universes, going back and forth among them."

The Lord said to Satan, "You have tempted Adam and Eve. I shall punish you according to each circumstance."

Satan tempted Adam and Eve and their descendants with the lust of the flesh, the lust of the eyes, and the pride of life. They traded their eternity for temporary gratification and they traded the truth for a lie!

God's Discussion with the Guardian Angels:

For Universe 1, The Guardian Angels said, "Lord we have done as you have commanded. We have gone to Universe 1 and provided all the support, guidance, and path to righteousness that we could to these people, however, they have shown themselves to be prone to sin. The people of Universe 1 have a proclivity for sin. Often, they want to do right, but somehow, they manage to still do the wrong thing." Since their father, Adam, was not a good example of a role model, they were trying to figure life out on their own and that would often lead to a bad outcome. Having a good father, father figure, or role model in your life makes a world of difference in your chance at life for success and salvation.

For Universe 2, The Guardian Angels said, "Lord we have done as you have commanded. We have gone to Universe 2 and provided all the support, guidance, and path to righteousness that we could to these people. They have shown that their hearts and minds are open to the path of righteousness, however, the path to righteousness is narrow and thin and the path for sin is wide and large. They have free will to make the choice for good or evil."

God said, "You have done as I have commanded, but continue to support and guide them. I want to provide every opportunity for them to reach their salvation and serve me here in the Kingdom of Heaven forever!"

So, the Guardian Angels did as God commanded and returned to Universe 1 and Universe 2.

God said to them, "What no eye has seen, what no ear has heard, and what no human mind has conceived the things God has prepared for those who love him. Follow God's word and it will be all right."

CPSIA information can be obtained
at www.ICGtesting.com
Printed in the USA
LVHW060942070323
740942LV00045B/575